The Trouble with Trent

A Comedy
by

Fred Carmichael

SAMUEL FRENCH, INC.

45 WEST 25TH STREET   NEW YORK 10010
7623 SUNSET BOULEVARD HOLLYWOOD 90046
LONDON   TORONTO

ISBN 0 573 62655 3   Printed in U.S.A.   # 22744

IMPORTANT BILLING AND CREDIT REQUIREMENTS

CAST OF CHARACTERS:

ALICE CROYDON

DD HAVERTY

LEORA FOXCROFT

OSSIE

ANGELA PLUNKETT

PHOEBE BAXTER

IRENE SMITHFIELD

KENNETH

ACT I:

A beach house on a Spring morning.
The present day.

ACT II:

Scene One: That evening.
Scene Two: Later at almost one o'clock.

ACT I

(The action of the play takes place in a rented beach cottage. D.R. is a bedroom door with a desk onstage of it with a swivel desk chair on the right of it and an upholstered bench center of it. The upstage wall is slanted to the left with a closet U.R. with the door hinged on the right. Directly center of this is a pair of French windows opening off stage and to the left is a bedroom door. Outside the windows are the walls of the closet and the bedroom and beyond this is a stone wall parallel to the room so one can go out and turn either L. or R. On the L. wall of the room is an arch which leads to the front door and rest of the cottage. Below this is another bedroom door. On stage of this is a large arm chair with a high hassock to the C. of it which can be used for sitting. C. stage there is a large round table with three chairs around it. The furniture is all light and airy with a decorator's touch obvious. There is a phone and a portable alarm clock on the desk. Any decor used depends on the size of the stage and perhaps plants and summer objects d'arts are seen. The time is 11:00 AM, the present.)

(At rise the stage is empty. The alarm clock on the desk rings and three women enter simultaneously. ALICE CROYDON, from R. is probably in her thirties, is attractive but at the moment has her hair pulled back and wears glasses which she uses or puts atop her head. From U.L. room LEORA FOXCROFT runs in. She is the oldest of the three and seems more efficient and tailored and is possibly an executive. From D.L. DD HAVERTY runs in. DD, always called by the two initials, is the youngest of the three and appears to be a bit more naive and innocent. They all have a wonderful comraderie and a mutual sense of humor although it is not based on a long-term relationship. The following dialogue overlaps.)

ALICE. *(Leans over the desk hitting the alarm clock so it stops.)* I've got it!

(Her purse is on the desk and she holds a pile of typed pages.)

DD. *(Runs on holding pile of typed pages)* Great timing. I just finished my part.

LEORA. I'm just clearing up the blood. What a murder!

ALICE. Sex. I'm telling you, that's what sells.

(Slaps papers on desk.)

LEORA. *(Moves C.)* You haven't overdone it have you?

ALICE. Read it and see.

DD. *(Crosses in to table)* I had trouble with that English garden but now I've got it. They do grow dianthus, don't they?

ALICE. Play it safe. Make them geraniums.

LEORA. Blood. I was going to write, 'Who would have thought the old man had so much blood in him' but someone beat me to it.

ALICE. Shakespeare.

LEORA. Bah, humbug.

ALICE. That was –

ALICE & LEORA. Charles Dickens.

LEORA. I know that.

DD. Stop it, you two. The clock went off. It is eleven A.M. and I'm putting my chapter down.

(Puts her papers on table.)

ALICE. But I'm right where Tarquin breaks down Kimberly's bedroom door.

LEORA. Does he hurt his shoulder?

ALICE. That wouldn't stop Tarquin.

DD. *(Goes to French windows)* Out to the beach, Alice. You can cool off.

ALICE. Right. If we don't stick to the rules we are lost.

LEORA. *(Goes to DD)* Why rent a beach house unless you use the beach?

DD. What number sun screen shall I use?

ALICE. *(Goes above desk)* Cut the screen. We won't be out long enough.

DD. *(Comes down)* How about taking the rest of the morning off?

ALICE. No way.

LEORA. *(Goes to DD)* I'll give you one very good reason.

DD. What?

LEORA. The IRS.

ALICE. We rent this for two weeks and it is deductible but only if we produce work.

LEORA. Are we all putting P.D. James to shame?

ALICE. That part where we catch the murderer is really so exciting. I can't believe we wrote it.

LEORA. Amazing we three get along so well and how we work together editing and adding to each other. It's like building a pyramid.

DD. I never thought people could collaborate so well.

ALICE. Except maybe Rodgers and Hammerstein.

LEORA. Sears and Roebuck.

DD. Mickey and Minnie.

LEORA. Who?

DD. The Mouses – Mice – oh, forget it.

ALICE. *(Goes out the French doors)* Come on, we're wasting our ocean-break time.

LEORA. You can't wait to get back into Kimberly's bedroom.

ALICE. Neither can Tarquin.

LEORA. I guess we have to thank the muses for technology.

DD. Why?

LEORA. *(As she exits)* We never would have met without technology.

ALICE. *(As she disappears out and to the R.)* Then thanks to our particular muse.

DD. *(As she follows them off)* Ours? Is there a muse of the Internet?

(Closet door opens and OSSIE poles his head out. OSSIE is probably in his forties and is a real beach bum complete with stubble, jeans, T-shirt, sandals and no socks. Crosses to the desk, opens ALICE's

purse and takes out a wallet and inside it a charge card and holds it up.)

OSSIE. Just my luck, gold and not platinum. *(Puts it back and brings out a money clip with bills on it)* Ah, this is better. *(Puts it in his pocket, looks through a page or two of the typed pages and picks up the alarm clock)* Wouldn't you know, Tiffany. *(Starts for windows, stops and looks at clock in hand)* Money, yes, clock, no.

(Starts back to desk as ANGIE PLUNKETT speaks from hallway.)

ANGIE. *(Off stage)* Hello. Leora!
OSSIE. Cripes!
ANGIE. Alice!
OSSIE. *(Realizes he is caught between doors and opens closet door)* This is a bad idea.

(Closes door as ANGIE enters.)

ANGIE. *(Enters)* Anyone home? *(ANGIE is a literary agent and has been traveling so she is more tailored than the others. She is somewhere in middleage and may seem austere but she is a very nice person. She carries a briefcase. She opens door L.)* Is one of you in here? *(Goes in leaving door open. OSSIE comes out of closet and is about to put the clock back on the desk when he hears her.)* Script, script, do I see a script? *(OSSIE ducks into ALICE's room as ANGIE comes out)* No luck in there. *(She puts briefcase on the hassock and sees U.L. room)* Another bedroom. *(Opens that door)* Ah, a lap top. Good girl. *(Goes in leaving door open as OSSIE enters and runs for French windows, realizes still has the clock in his hand and turns as ANGIE speaks)* Aha, the pot of gold! *(OSSIE ducks into the closet as ANGIE enters with typed pages and crosses to desk)* More script. My cup runneth over with nouns and adjectives. *(Sits in desk chair and swivels front reading as OSSIE comes out of closet, puts the clock on the desk and exits windows)* Not only nouns and adjectives but subjunctive clauses. Now all I need to see is a suspenseful plot. *(Swivels around and sees the clock)* Eleven o'clock. Why aren't they working? *(Picks up clock)* Hm, Tiffany. Does this come with the house?

PHOEBE. No, it does not.

(PHOEBE BAXTER stands in the arch. She is in summer business clothes and holds a tote bag. She is somewhat older than ANGIE and appears a bit flighty but very sincere.)

ANGIE. I beg your pardon.

PHOEBE. Oh, dear, I didn't mean to be so abrupt.

ANGIE. I didn't intent to steal the clock.

PHOEBE. *(Crosses C.)* I'm sure the last tenant left it here. *(With a broad smile)* You use it in good health. That's what we think of you.

ANGIE. I'm at a loss for words.

PHOEBE. Imagine me barging in like this but the door was open. You must have guessed who I am?

ANGIE. Well, I –

PHOEBE. 'Fess up now, you did guess I'm Phoebe Baxter now, didn't you?

ANGIE. I'm usually so good at Twenty Questions.

PHOEBE. But then you didn't deal with me directly at the office.

ANGIE. What – which office?

PHOEBE. 'Sun and Sand Rentals' of course.

ANGIE. *(Rises and goes above desk to PHOEBE)* I am now putting it together, Ms. Baxter, slowly but it is coming into focus. You have dropped in to be sure this beach house is comfortable and convenient for us.

PHOEBE. I know the office opened up for you but I wanted to check in and be sure everything was hunky-dory.

ANGIE. Hunky-dory. That's the word.

PHOEBE. *(Grabs ANGIE's hand and shakes it eagerly)* It is such a privilege to rent to you and I couldn't let the chance slip by to meet you in person and here you are.

ANGIE. Here I am.

PHOEBE. Now one little favor and then I'll dash.

ANGIE. Anything to help you on your way.

PHOEBE. *(Pulls a book from her tote bag)* If you'll just sign this for me.

ANGIE. *(Looks at it)* I'd be delighted but I am not Dr. Seuss.

PHOEBE. Oh, dear. This is for my niece and I must have left 'The Mail Is Black' at home. Silly me. *(Goes to arch)* I'll go back for it.

ANGIE. Along with not being Dr. Seuss, I am also not the author of 'The Mail Is Black'.

PHOEBE. *(Turns)* You are not Sarah Trent?

ANGIE. I'd be delighted to sign this book Angela Plunkett.

PHOEBE. What must you think of me?

ANGIE. I plead the fifth.

PHOEBE. The what?

ANGIE. I am Angela Plunkett and I am the literary agent for Sarah Trent.

PHOEBE. *(Moves in)* You do contracts, foreign rights, residuals? I read about those mega-buck deals.

ANGIE. Sarah Trent is not quite in that league yet.

PHOEBE. But close?

ANGIE. *(With a secretive smile as she sits R. of table)* About to be ever so much closer.

PHOEBE. Are you staying here with Sarah Trent?

ANGIE. No. I just dropped my bags off two houses down the beach at that B and B.

PHOEBE. Naturally you can't stay here, not when Sarah Trent is working, not when she reaches for her pen and –

ANGIE. No pen.

PHOEBE. Computer?

ANGIE. Lap top.

PHOEBE. No one thought she could track down that blackmailer in 'The Mail Is Black' and against all odds she did it. *(Sits L. of table)* Tell me, I know some of the book must be fiction but the real Sarah Trent must have a lot of the book Sarah Trent in her. I mean she seems so young and willing and – and –

ANGIE. Able?

PHOEBE. Yes, able. So very able. She is like her books, isn't she?

ANGIE. It really wouldn't be fair for me to pull away the veil of the mystique.

PHOEBE. How beautiful – the veil of the mystique.

ANGIE. I stole it from Robert Louis Stevenson.

PHOEBE. *(Rises)* Where is she? If I could have just one glimpse of Sarah Trent.

ANGIE. *(Rises and guides PHOEBE towards the arch)* Maybe later when you change Dr. Seuss for 'The Mail Is Black'.

PHOEBE. Of course. It's been so nice to meet you, Ms –

ANGIE. Plunkett.

PHOEBE. Plunkett, I must get your autograph, too, some time or other. *(As she turns in the arch a woman backs in quietly. She is middleaged but very sophisticated looking, dressed in dark clothes with huge sun glasses. She is IRENE SMITHFIELD. PHOEBE watches her, all enthusiasm)* Sarah Trent, it is you!

IRENE. *(Turns to face them)* No, no, not Sarah Trent. Not her. I wish I were. The door was open. I'll go but this is the right place, isn't it? Sarah Trent is here?

PHOEBE. No.

ANGIE. Yes.

PHOEBE. Not right at the moment.

ANGIE. Can I help you?

IRENE. Are you Sarah Trent?

PHOEBE. No.

ANGIE. No, I am her literary agent.

IRENE. Then you are Angela Plunkett.

ANGIE. Yes.

PHOEBE. *(Crosses below them to C.)* I must see Sarah Trent. I am –

PHOEBE. Everyone wants to see Sarah Trent.

IRENE. I have come all the way from Washington, D.C. and –

ANGIE. You're not, you can't be – ?

IRENE. I am Irene –

ANGIE. *(Obviously interrupting)* But how do you know Sarah Trent is here?

IRENE. Internet.

ANGIE. Damn machine.

PHOEBE. You can find out anything on the Internet if you look long enough. The one at the office has –

IRENE. Where is she? The envelope, I mailed her an envelope.

ANGIE. *(Goes to her)* It arrived safely.

IRENE. *(Sinks onto the bench by the desk)* It's all too dangerous. My nerves are frazzling.

PHOEBE. *(Excited, she crosses in)* Is it about a new book, a thriller?

ANGIE. *(Goes to IRENE)* Miss – er – Irene, why don't you go and – are you in a car?

IRENE. Rented. Chevrolet. Airport.

ANGIE. *(Pulls her up and takes her to the arch)* Then why don't you take a drive down the beach. It's beautiful and restful. You can unfrazzle those nerves while I talk to Sarah Trent and I know everything will work out satisfactorily.

PHOEBE. I'm sure Sarah Trent can solve whatever it is.

IRENE. *(Turns on her)* How do you know?

ANGIE. She doesn't, but I do. Trust me. *(Ushers her out)* You take a spin, eat a hot dog, salt water taffy, something, and then come back.

IRENE. She is my last hope. If Sarah Trent can't help, it's me for the ocean.

(Exits)

ANGIE. *(Calls after her)* Drive carefully.

PHOEBE. I never know whether to take out extra insurance on a rental. What do you do?

ANGIE. Frankly my mind right now is not on car insurance.

PHOEBE. That woman. Mysterious. Does Sarah Trent get many mysteries to solve?

ANGIE. Hundreds, and now *(Gets her to the arch)* I must get to work on this one. You and Dr. Seuss run along.

PHOEBE. Tell Sarah Trent I shall return felt tip in hand.

(Exits)

ANGIE. *(Comes back in, goes to briefcase on hassock, takes out large stuffed envelope which is addressed and stamped)* Irene Smithfield, Washington, D.C. A return address on something like this? She is crazy.

DD. *(Off stage)* Hurry up, you'll be baked like a potato. I should have put on sun screen.

LEORA. *(Off stage)* For ten minutes?

ALICE. An egg is done in three.

DD. *(Off stage)* Look at these freckles. *(Comes in and sees ANGIE)* Oh.

ANGIE. Hello.

DD. *(Goes to her)* You're from the rental office, right?

ANGIE. No, she just left. You must be Alice Croydon.

DD. No, I'm DD Haverty and tell me who you are before I call someone.

ANGIE. Who? Alice or Leora?

DD. You know too much. You're either a physic or an alien.

ANGIE. Or an agent. I am Angie Plunkett.

DD. You're? – we meet – it's really you – you're here – why? What's happened? I must tell the others.

(Runs to windows.)

ANGIE. *(To herself)* I'm happy to meet you, too.

DD. *(Calls)* Hey, guess who's here.

LEORA. *(Off stage)* Jimmy Hoffa?

ALICE. *(Off stage)* Interview him and we'll get another book.

DD. No, it is Angela Plunkett.

LEORA. *(Off stage)* Here?

DD. Yes. *(Comes back to ANGIE)* Does anyone else know you're here?

ANGIE. I'm the only one who knows the truth about Sarah Trent.

LEORA. *(Rushes in followed by ALICE)* Where is she? Where is the genius woman?

ANGIE. *(Goes below DD to C.)* That must be me. You're Leora?

LEORA. Yes. It is absolutely marvelous to finally meet you.

ANGIE. *(Goes to ALICE)* That leaves the third musketeer, Alice Croydon.

ALICE. *(They shake hands)* It is my pleasure, believe me. *(To others)* Did you know she was coming? Is this a surprise?

LEORA. She's news to me.

DD. I couldn't have kept this secret.

ALICE. Oh, hell, we should have been working.

DD. We have been, honest.

LEORA. We only took a ten minute break. The new book is almost finished.

ANGIE. I'm not checking up on you. *(Picks up briefcase and sits in chair L.)* I'm here to bring news.

ALICE. Good or bad?

ANGIE. Let's just say it is news.

ALICE. We've hit the Times best-seller list?

ANGIE. Not quite.

DD. Movies? You've had an offer?

LEORA. *(Goes C.)* Will you two calm down and be reasonable.

DD. Leora's the sensible Sarah Trent.

LEORA. Sensible enough to offer you some coffee. The pot is on.

ANGIE. You'll need caffeine for what I'm going to tell you.

LEORA. *(Starts for arch)* I'll get it.

DD. No, let me. *(To ANGIE)* I am the domestic Sarah Trent, the one who knows housework, gardening and arranging flowers Japanese style.

ALICE. A good hostess would ask if anyone else wanted coffee.

DD. *(Overly polite)* Does anyone else wish coffee?

ALICE. *(Triumphantly)* No.

DD. What?

ALICE. No – thank you.

LEORA. I will and black as usual.

ANGIE. Same for me.

DD. Then no saucers. You'll each get a mug. That's what Sarah Trent would do.

(Exits arch.)

LEORA. But only in DD's rewrites.

ALICE. *(Sits on the bench)* Combine Martha Stewart and Dear Abby and you have DD.

ANGIE. If she is the domestic one and, Leora, you are the sensible one then that leaves Alice to be the – the – how shall I put it – the –

ALICE. The sexy one?

ANGIE. You put it very well.

ALICE. But only on the page.

LEORA. *(Sits R. of table)* So she claims but we know nothing about her.

ANGIE. *(Rises and puts briefcase on table)* Then it is true? You haven't been pulling my leg. You really do not know each other very well?

LEORA. Hardly at all. Isn't it marvelous?

ANGIE. Incredible.

LEORA. So we have no personality conflicts, no hang-ups.

ALICE. But we write well together as you know but only by mail.

LEORA. Or FAX.

ALICE. But if we shared our lives together I'm sure we would hate each other.

LEORA. *(Smiles)* Perhaps.

ALICE. *(Smiles back)* Probably.

DD. *(Stands in arch with 2 mugs of coffee)* Definitely.

ANGIE. Really?

DD. *(Gives mugs to ANGIE and LEORA)* I'm sure of it. Leora would be insufferably smart about everything.

LEORA. It's my strong point.

DD. And from Alice's writing she would be mistress of the mayor and live a back street life.

ALICE. So I put some steam into Sarah Trent's life. That doesn't mean I'm that way myself and what about you, Miss Goody-Two-Shoes?

ANGIE. *(Laughs as she sits L. of table)* I haven't heard that expression since kindergarten.

DD. *(Goes above table)* Just because I know the niceties of life like gardening, furniture styles, glassware and such –

LEORA. She is the descriptive Sarah Trent.

ANGIE. But that's one of the big selling points with book clubs, the way the style is slyly written in.

DD. There, you see.

ALICE. *(Barely a whispered sing-song)* There is a reason she is called DD.

ANGIE. What *does* it stand for?

ALICE. Go on, tell her.

DD. Mother says she has seen every movie Doris Day ever made.

(Throws her hands up as she sinks on the hassock.)

LEORA. Can you blame DD's mother for wanting a baby with a sunny disposition always bouncing around doing good?

ALICE. Of course DD could stand for Doris Duke.

LEORA. No, she was a poor little rich girl. How about Dead-eye Dick?

ALICE. Was he real or fictional?

DD. It could be Daffy Duck.

ANGIE. But your name is really Doris Day?

DD. Doris Day Haverty but everyone *(Glares at the others)* – I mean *everyone* calls me DD.

ALICE. And I bet her house is so clean it squeaks.

DD. I don't live in a house. I live in an apartment.

ALICE. Penthouse?

LEORA. *(Rises)* Stop, both of you right there. Remember our bargain. We agreed not to know anything about each other's lives. Now we know DD lives in an apartment.

DD. Sorry, I forgot.

ALICE. I broke the rules but then my Sarah Trent is always breaking the rules.

ANGIE. You really do not know anything about each other?

LEORA. Nothing. Nada. Zilch.

ANGIE. And yet you three make Sarah Trent such a real woman.

LEORA. *(Goes above table to L.)* Maybe she is the better part of each of us.

ALICE. Or the subconscious part.

DD. *(To ALICE)* Your subconscious part would embarrass Lady Chatterly.

ANGIE. You three are unbelievable. I don't even know why I read your book when it showed up at the agency. I usually don't bother with scripts from unknowns.

LEORA. You must have gotten hooked right off.

ALICE. That's because I put some sex in the second paragraph.

ANGIE. Whatever it was I kept reading. I must say the suspense started quickly and never let up.

LEORA. That's a combined effort but the more technical part, that is mine.

DD. Leora takes care of any machine questions ranging from car motors to bombs.

ALICE. I suspect she's a big executive for the government and others do the research for her.

LEORA. You'll never know.

ANGIE. But three authors for me to answer and three addresses, what was I to think?

ALICE. You must have flipped when you realized Sarah Trent was three people.

ANGIE. Surprised is a better word.

DD. *(Rises and goes to her)* Your suggestions were great. I didn't know agents were such good editors.

ANGIE. Publishers know what the market wants so that's what we have to give them. *(With her cup)* Say, this is really great coffee. Which of you made it?

ALICE & LEORA. *(As DD smiles)* Doris Day Haverty, who else.

DD. Combination of Sumatra and Tanzania beans.

ALICE. You had to ask.

ANGIE. *(Rises and goes to ALICE at desk)* There is so much I don't know about you. How did you all meet anyway, a writer's conference or what?

ALICE. No way. I'm not one to stand in front of other writers and read my work.

LEORA. *(Sits chair D.L.)* I'd read a short mystery piece Alice had written in a magazine and it so involved me I thought I'd write my first fan letter.

ALICE. Flatterer.

ANGIE. How nice.

LEORA. I wormed Alice's address out of the Internet. It took a bit of searching bit it can be done.

ANGIE. Those damn machines.

DD. *(Sits L. of table)* But your news? Talk about suspense. What is our news?

ANGIE. *(Sits on the hassock)* First tell me how they found you?

DD. I've always wanted to be a mystery writer and I wrote a one act play our women's club put on.

ALICE. *(Rises and crosses in) Your* women's club? Did you get that, Leora, now we know she's part of a club for all women. Tea and chatter.

LEORA. That's no surprise.

DD. I let the cat out of the bag.

LEORA. DD is also master of the chiché.

DD. My play was good enough to be published, cliché-ridden or not.

LEORA. And it had something so different about it, so suspenseful and yet so simple and direct.

ALICE. Did you see it at a women's club?

LEORA. Ha! A library. The play was about a small town and the crime in it involved the people and their way of life.

DD. Miss Marple may have inspired me a tiny bit.

LEORA. The Internet brought up her address and we actually started talking.

ALICE. *(Sits R. of table)* And they got ahold of me and we three made up our own chat room as they say.

DD. And it was – yes, it was you, Leora, who first said we should work together.

LEORA. It seemed so far out I thought it might work.

ALICE. I was sure I couldn't work with anyone else and then my daytime job –

DD. *(Warning her)* Uh-uh.

ALICE. – of which I shall not speak. Anyway, how could we work together so far apart?

LEORA. We chattered away on our computers and came up with the beginning outline for a murder plot. *(Goes below table to ALICE)* I said I'd send a short, rough draft to Alice.

ALICE. I expanded on it and added my spicy bits and shipped it off to DD.

DD. And I added my own ideas and gave it some style.

LEORA. *(Goes to desk)* Then it came back to me and I added some of my technical know-how and juiced up the suspense.

(Sits on bench.)

ALICE. It kept being passed around and got more and more exciting until we knew we had to meet.

DD. Which we did last year.

ALICE. I rented a house for us in the mountains and we worked solidly for two weeks polishing "The Mail Is Black' into shape.

DD. The big danger was that three women together would chatter the time away talking about ourselves so we made rule number one.

LEORA. Which is to stick to the book and keep each of us a mystery to the other two.

ALICE. *(Rises and goes to ANGIE)* We looked through lists of agents and you seemed to handle some reasonably well-known mystery authors so you got it.

ANGIE. Amazing, utterly amazing.

LEORA. This year we decided on the beach for our two weeks and the new book is almost ready for your approval and editing.

ANGIE. *(Nervously paces to R. of desk)* It's still in the first person I hope.

ALICE. Yes. Sarah Trent lives on.

ANGIE. She was such a hit with the readers and they're clambering for more.

ALICE. You were so right telling us to kill off her husband and leave her to go it alone.

ANGIE. You should see the hundreds of sympathy cards Sarah Trent received. You ought to get a finder's fee from Hallmark.

DD. Sympathy for the heroine. That auto accident was my idea.

ALICE. But cut brake lining has been so over-used we threw the problem to Leora.

LEORA. And I went with that electrical malfunction.

ANGIE. Great idea but Sarah Trent does recover quickly?

ALICE. After a brief fling with her handsome therapist.

ANGIE. I can't wait to read it.

LEORA. Then don't keep us talking. What kind of agent are you?

ANGIE. First there is this problem.

DD. Finally your news.

ANGIE. I'm afraid I've been a bit over-zealous.

LEORA. How over-zealous?

ANGIE. *(Moves above table)* Your first book has been doing very well but why do others which are not as good hit it so big?

DD. Better plotting perhaps?

ANGIE. No, it's because they are true. Remember Truman Capote's 'In Cold Blood'?

ALICE. And what about 'Midnight in the Garden of Good and Evil'? On the best-seller list for years.

ANGIE. Because they were based on true people.

LEORA. I think I know what you are leading up to.

ALICE. I have that same feeling.

DD. I am completely lost.

ANGIE. *(Moves to R. of table)* All I did was say in one interview how exciting true mysteries are. The reporter asked if 'The Mail Is Black' was true and I smiled ever so subtly. Then he asked if Sarah Trent was real. I said something non-committal like 'could be' which he took to mean 'definitely is' and the media picked it up from there.

DD. But there is no Sarah Trent.

ANGIE. *(Sinks on the hassock)* There is now.

ALICE. This beats 'The Three Faces of Eve' all hollow.

LEORA. *(Rises and goes above DD at table L.)* We've just given birth.

ALICE. Should we hand out cigars?

ANGIE. You understand we have stumbled on some great publicity. Sales from the first book and whatever this new one is will go through the roof.

LEORA. *(Goes to ANGIE)* But only as long as Sarah Trent is real?

ANGIE. Exactly.

ALICE. Real for how long?

ANGIE. Until the next book is out and then introducing all of you will be another literary bombshell.

DD. Then your news is all good.

ANGIE. *(Rises and goes below them to the desk)* All except there is this problem. It's not my fault really but I did say you were real so some of the blame –

DD. Stop beating about the bush.

LEORA. Thank God for DD's chichés.

ALICE. Out with it. What's the problem?

IRENE. *(Is standing in arch)* I am!

LEORA. I should have said, 'Who is the problem?'

ANGIE. Irene, you're back.

ALICE. *(Rises)* From where and who are you?

IRENE. Silly me.

LEORA. That's a big help.

ANGIE. I was just about to tell them about the mix-up.

IRENE. Mix-up? Fifty thousand dollars is no mix-up.

LEORA. I am getting intrigued.

ALICE. *(Sits on the bench)* Moi, aussi.

ANGIE. I was just starting to tell them –

IRENE. Them? *(Crosses by L. of table)* No, no, only Sarah Trent can help me.

ANGIE. But she is here.

IRENE. Well, which of you is Sarah Trent? *(Pause as they look at each other)* All right then, Sarah Trent, you stay! You other two leave the room. Now!

(They all turn to go.)

ANGIE. Don't go! *(They stop)* Believe me, Irene, one of them is Sarah Trent.

IRENE. Well, which? Speak up!

ANGIE. *(Moves below desk)* It's best you don't know, that no one knows. She's playing it very low-profile. Fans, autograph seekers, she is always besieged and, of course, there is the constant danger.

DD. Danger?

ANGIE. Of past criminals she has caught. Once they're out of prison they may come after her.

IRENE. *(Goes to ANGIE)* Of course, but can't I know which of them is Sarah Trent?

ANGIE. Tell them your problem and perhaps the real Sarah Trent will agree to help.

IRENE. I don't know how to begin. Silly, stupid me.

DD. I love alliteration. Silly, stupid.

LEORA. Get to it, the fifty thousand dollars.

ANGIE. To begin with, this is Irene Smithfield.

LEORA. Obviously a fake name.

IRENE. I thought it sounded so non-commital.

ALICE. Go ahead and commit now.

IRENE. *(To ANGIE)* Must I tell all?

ANGIE. You had better.

(Leans back on desk to listen.)

IRENE. It was to be a weekend in Virginia, an illicit weekend.

ALICE. Ah, my territory. By illicit you mean love nest?

LEORA. You said, 'was to be'. It didn't come off?

IRENE. Not quite.

ALICE. Drat!

IRENE. A man I had been seeing socially, also quietly –

DD. Who?

IRENE. That I will not tell ever. He is very prominent and – well, you must not know his name. *(Sits on bench)* He made arrangements for this weekend and slipped a note into my hand at one of those Washington charity functions.

DD. How was the room decorated?

LEORA. *(Warning her)* DD.

DD. Sorry. Continue.

IRENE. The note said where we were to meet and also had a few words of endearment.

ALICE. Never put anything in writing.

IRENE. I read it quickly in the ladies room and slipped it into my pocket. When I got to my car it was gone. Someone had picked my pocket.

LEORA. Who?

IRENE. How could I tell? You know how crowded those parties are, wall-to-wall people.

DD. One should never invite more guests than the space can comfortably accommodate.

IRENE. The next day I was contacted by a blackmailer.

ALICE. Your friend, too?

IRENE. No and I couldn't tell him. He would definitely not approve and would track this person down and ruin him.

DD. How?

IRENE. Quietly I know. An IRS audit, a trumped up drug charge, who knows? But it would bring my name into the open and ruin me socially.

DD. This I can understand.

IRENE. I can't have that and since money is no object –

LEORA. *(Sits on hassock)* Remember that line, 'money is no object'. I like it.

ANGIE. Get to the present.

IRENE. I withdrew the money from the bank.

LEORA. This is where the fifty thousand comes in?

IRENE. Yes. *(Rises and goes above table)* I carefully put it in an envelope to send to the post office box number I was given.

LEORA. You sent fifty thousand dollars without even registering it?

IRENE. In large bills.

ALICE. Thick envelope, wasn't it?

IRENE. Anyone would have thought it was a catalog or one of those entries from the Publisher's Clearing House.

DD. I never win anything.

IRENE. *(Goes to L. of table)* But at the same time I did a dreadful, stupid thing.

DD. Silly, stupid thing?

IRENE. Yes. I had written a short mystery story in my spare time and I had read your wonderful book and I wanted your opinion of it so I sent it off to you but –

(Stops)

LEORA. You didn't?

ALICE. How could you?

DD. Did what?

LEORA. She mailed the story to the blackmailer and the fifty thousand to Sarah Trent.

DD. *(After a stunned silence during which IRENE nods her head)* You're right, silly, stupid you.

ANGIE. *(Rises and goes above table)* It came to Sarah Trent at my office. It was even postage due.

IRENE. Sorry about that.

ANGIE. I assumed it was a script from some crank – sorry, Irene.

IRENE. I can take it.

ANGIE. I opened the envelope.

DD. Did you scream?

ANGIE. My secretary wanted to call 911.

LEORA. Where is the fifty thousand now?

ALICE. In large bills.

ANGIE. *(Takes large envelope from attaché case on table)* Here.

LEORA. And her short story is in the hands of the blackmailer?

IRENE. He put a message on the Internet for me.

DD. What did it say?

IRENE. That my story wasn't very good.

DD. That's all?

IRENE. Also that he would meet me here at Sarah Trent's and hand over the note when I give him the money.

ALICE. How did he know Sarah Trent was here?

IRENE. The Internet and Ms. Plunkett's secretary.

ANGIE. I'll speak to her. *(Goes R. of table)* So that's where we are. One blackmailer, one victim, one authoress, and fifty thousand dollars.

IRENE. *(Rises)* He'll show up with the note, I'll pay him and it will be over. So, if you will just give me the money.

(Puts her hand out.)

LEORA. *(Rises and goes C.)* Just a minute. Angie is not going to hand over all that money to a perfect stranger.

ALICE. *(Rises)* What if you're the blackmailer and you're trying to get the money?

IRENE. But I am Irene Smithfield.

DD. You admitted it wasn't your real name.

IRENE. I know but I am who I am and I don't want you to know who I am.

ANGIE. *(Picks up case, puts envelope back in it and goes to desk)* I had better keep this.

DD. Should we call the FBI or someone?

IRENE. I already called them. They wouldn't help unless they knew the right names of the people and, of course, I couldn't tell them who I am.

LEORA. Did you call them from home?

IRENE. Yes, but –

LEORA. Of course they traced the call. They know who you really are and I'm sure one of them is here right now. *(Sits chair R. of table)* I happen to know about such things.

ALICE. Do you?

IRENE. You're smart. I'm sure you are Sarah Trent.

ALICE. You think she has the passion of Sarah Trent?

DD. Or the stylish knowledge?

IRENE. *(Goes to chair L.)* I don't know. It's all too confusing. I just want to get that incriminating note and return to my garden, my jacuzzi, and my croquet lawn.

DD. *(Goes to her)* Do you grow dianthus?

IRENE. Di-what?

DD. Dianthus. If you're a gardener you should know dianthus.

IRENE. My man does the gardening. I just admire.

ALICE. *(Sits on bench)* I admire my geranium on a windowsill.

LEORA. So no outdoor garden? Then you live in an apartment.

ALICE. Or I have a large kitchen window in a large house.

ANGIE. *(Goes to IRENE)* Why don't you go back to your croquet lawn and let us do the trading?

IRENE. And leave my fifty thousand here?

DD. You said it was only money.

IRENE. *(To ANGIE)* How do I know it it's in that envelope? It could be just ripped up newspaper.

ALICE. That's right. We haven't seen the cold cash.

LEORA. Show us the cash.

ANGIE. *(Rises and takes envelope to above the table)* Is there no trust among us?

LEORA. None. Open that envelope.

ANGIE. *(They all rush to look inside it as she opens it)* Here you are, fifty thousand dollars.

ALICE. It's so green.

DD. I thought it would look somehow more impressive.

ALICE. We trust you. *(Goes above desk. To others)* Think it over, she must be the genuine Angela Plunkett because she knew the whole beginning of Sarah Trent. Right, girls?

DD. *(Sits L. of table)* Yes.

LEORA. *(Sits on bench)* Agreed.

IRENE. Then what am I to do, sit and wait till someone says, 'Here is the note, where is the money?'

LEORA. No. It's very difficult to arrange a pick-up. He'll wonder if you've contacted the authorities and federal agents are around and about.

ALICE. You can discuss it all you want but I have Tarquin going into Kimberly's bedroom and she is an important woman.

(Heads for her room.)

IRENE. Tarquin? Kimberly? Are other people here?

ALICE. No, it's just a trashy book I'm reading.

ANGIE. *(Goes to IRENE)* Irene, why don't we go over to my place and these girls can get on with whatever it is they're doing.

LEORA. Yes, we have things to complete.

IRENE. What if the blackmailer shows up?

LEORA. We'll send him over.

IRENE. *(Sits on hassock)* No, I had better stay here.

ANGIE. *(Picks up her briefcase)* As you wish. If you want me, I'm just two doors down that way.

(Starts out window.)

DD. *(To IRENE)* There she goes with your fifty thousand.

LEORA. Suppose she's your blackmailer. She has the money and you don't have your note.

IRENE. Angela Plunkett is a respected agent, isn't she?

ALICE. If she *is* Angela Plunkett.

IRENE. Sarah Trent would know her own agent, wouldn't she? *(Rises and looks at the three)* Wouldn't you?

DD. Who are you talking to?

IRENE. Whichever of you is Sarah Trent. Which? Speak up.

ALICE. You know we can't.

DD. You'd better follow that envelope but then, of course, the money is no object.

IRENE. *(Goes to window)* If I'm not back in fifteen minutes call the police, an ambulance, send a St. Bernard.

(Exits)

DD. She thinks she's in the Alps thirsting for a drink.

LEORA. I'm not in the Alps but I am thirsting for something.

ALICE. We deserve a double something.

DD. How strong? It's still daylight.

ALICE. Close the windows, set your watch ahead and get us a drink.

DD. But our writing deadline? I'll get something but it will be diet.

(Exits arch.)

LEORA. I bet you ten dollars she has a catering business.

ALICE. *(Sits in desk chair)* I'm sure her home is spotless and drips chintz.

LEORA. Maybe she's married. Children? How do we know?

ALICE. No. Women with children can't resist dragging out photos. I don't know why, all babies look alike.

LEORA. Obviously you are not a mother.

ALICE. Are you?

LEORA. Remember the rule.

ALICE. When this book is finished let's confess all and let our hair down.

LEORA. 'Let our hair down'? And you talk about DD and her homilies.

ALICE. I'd love to know more about you.

LEORA. Maybe you wouldn't like me. Maybe I am morally rotten.

ALICE. Now you interest me. How rotten might you be?

LEORA. I could steam stamps off envelopes and reuse them. I

could park in the handicap zone at the supermarket. I could even slip food coupons out of newspapers without buying them.

ALICE. That is not what I call immoral.

LEORA. I could also kick cats and dogs.

ALICE. You wouldn't?

LEORA. *(Smiles)* No, I love animals, especially dogs.

ALICE. When my little Chloe was sick, I –

LEORA. Stop right there. You're telling too much. For all I know Chloe could be either a daughter or a dog.

ALICE. You want a hint? She has distemper.

DD. *(Comes in with three glasses of clear liquid)* Who has distemper? It could be catching.

LEORA. Never mind.

DD. *(Goes above desk, puts tray down and hands glasses around)* Here's our diet drink. Have you been telling secrets while I was out of the room?

ALICE. After this book is finished we ought to get together, have a party and finally trade biographies.

DD. That would be great. I'm dying to tell you about –

LEORA. What?

DD. *(Moves away to table)* No, it must wait.

ALICE. What was all that dianthus bit with Irene?

DD. Just checking if she knew garden flowers.

LEORA. Clever but she wangled out of it.

DD. Gardener indeed.

ALICE. *(Having tasted drink)* This is water.

DD. Diet spring water. It has absolutely nothing in it.

LEORA. And I can taste every bit of the nothing.

DD. *(Glances out windows)* I hope that Irene woman caught up with Angie.

ALICE. And the fifty thousand.

DD. Do you believe that blackmail story? Maybe Angie put her up to it to give us a plot.

LEORA. Sarah Trent already did blackmail.

DD. *(Moves down)* But now she is real. Sarah Trent lives.

ALICE. Which is why Irene Smithfield came to her – to us.

DD. Lucky we didn't write about the bubonic plague.

LEORA. If there is a blackmailer coming here with the now-infamous note –

ALICE. There must be. We saw the fifty thousand, didn't we? That's not just idle shopping money.

LEORA. And it seems some government agent is here, too.

ALICE. We're getting in over our collective heads already with Sarah Trent being alive.

LEORA. We should finish the new book and get out of here.

ALICE. In the meantime trust no one.

LEORA. We can't tell the good guys from the bad guys.

DD. The bad guys wear black hats.

LEORA. That went out with Hop-A-Long Cassidy.

DD. *(Sits above table)* On TV when you don't know the murderer just wait and ten minutes before the end whoever starts wearing black is guilty. It never fails.

ALICE. When I get home I shall throw out my basic little black dress.

LEORA. *(Rises)* Do any of us have much more work to do? Alice, I think you should make that bedroom scene longer.

ALICE. Any longer and we'll be banned in Boston.

DD. Why only in Boston?

LEORA. *(Goes to window)* It's just a phrase.

DD. I'm making that garden more overgrown and ominous, creeping, croaking frogs among the dianthus and all that. More suspenseful when Sarah's left alone with the murderer and she has to push him down onto the sundial.

LEORA. *(Goes down and sits table L.)* You're something and you did come up with the most unique murder weapon yet.

ALICE. *(Goes below desk to table)* It must come from living in the country.

DD. All murders don't have to be city-bred.

LEORA. But however did you think this one up?

DD. It was in the newspaper.

ALICE. *(Sits table R.)* You kid?

DD. Some farmer put the substance into his wife's IV when she was in the hospital.

LEORA. But water from his pond?

DD. Full of bacteria. Took the doctors ages to pinpoint it. She almost died.

LEORA. Great idea so keep up your subscription to whatever paper it is. *(Rises)* Now to work.

DD. Yes and fast.

(Moves towards her room.)

OSSIE. *(Stands in French windows and then moves in R.)* 'Scuse me.

ALICE. *(Goes up to him)* No, we don't want any.

OSSIE. Any what?

ALICE. Of whatever you're hawking. We only rent. Thanks anyway.

OSSIE. You don't want nothin'?

ALICE. No.

LEORA. Yes! *(Goes to him)* Maybe we do.

OSSIE. O.K.

(Continues to stand there.)

DD. I wish he was wearing a hat. Then we'd know.

OSSIE. Don't own no hat.

LEORA. Come on, out with it. Do you have that hand-written note?

OSSIE. Don't got no note. Don't even got a pencil.

LEORA. Then why are you here?

OSSIE. Money.

ALICE. I knew it.

LEORA. How much?

OSSIE. Here, you count it.

(Takes out money clip he took from her purse.)

ALICE. But that looks like – *(Takes it)* It's mine.

OSSIE. Could be.

ALICE. Where did you get it?

OSSIE. Lyin' in the sand by that wall out there.

ALICE. I must have dropped it when we walked down to the store. I'm always putting money in small pockets and I shouldn't. *(Takes a bill from the clip)* Here, take this reward.

OSSIE. Nope. Couldn't. Matter of principle.

DD. How nice.

LEORA. How original.

ALICE. You live around here? *(Looks at his dress)* No, of course not. You work around here? Guess not. What do you do?

OSSIE. I am a beach bum.

LEORA. No one says he is a beach bum.

OSSIE. I do. Just said it.

DD. What does a beach bum do?

OSSIE. *(Goes below LEORA to DD)* I work the beach, find cans, bottles, sometimes, like today, money. Folks hire me for small jobs when I'm not drunk. I just finished my last New York State muscatel. *(Looks at glass DD is holding)* Could I maybe have some of that white wine you're drinkin'?

DD. It is non-alcoholic, fat-free, tasteless diet water.

OSSIE. You pay for that with hard earned cash?

DD. It is cheaper than Scotch.

LEORA. But nowhere near as good.

OSSIE. Tell you what I'll do, Miss. I'll just take that reward you offered and get me a small bottle of non-diet but alcoholic wine down to the store.

ALICE. Of course. *(Gives him back a bill)* Is that enough?

OSSIE. Looks like plenty.

ALICE. Keep the change. *(Laughs)* I have never said that before.

OSSIE. I'll come by later and give you the change.

ALICE. From the wine?

OSSIE. Yep and maybe you'll have some chores for me. More chores, more wine. You be careful what you leave lyin' about out there. Next bum might not be as honest as me.

(Exits)

LEORA. I don't believe it.

DD. You mean 'I don't believe it' real or sarcastic?

LEORA. What do you think?

DD. He did find Alice's money, didn't he?

LEORA. *(Moves down)* And returned it. That's what I don't believe.

DD. Alice, what about you?

ALICE. *(With a smile she sits above table)* You missed a clue. I am the best detective of the Sarah Trents.

DD. What clue?

ALICE. I am the only one who got close enough to notice.

LEORA. Notice what?

ALICE. He just finished a bottle of cheap wine and he is looking for more, right?

DD. Right.

ALICE. Then why didn't his breath smell of wine?

LEORA. That's been used in too many stories.

DD. But this is real and it works.

LEORA. If you say anything about art imitating life I shall hit you.

ALICE. Then he is the blackmailer.

DD. *(Sits table L.)* He didn't ask for the money.

LEORA. Maybe he was casing us out to be sure we haven't called in the Feds.

DD. That sounds so good, Leora. The Feds.

ALICE. What are we going to do?

LEORA. *(Sits table R.)* What can we do? The fifty thousand is two doors down the beach so if anyone shows up with a note for sale we'll send him down there.

ALICE. Which means we can do what we do best which is?

ALL THREE. *(They all rise)* Work!

(Each starts for her own room.)

DD. I'll finish up that bit in the ninth chapter and I'm through.

ALICE. I'll get –

LEORA. We know, Tarquin and Kimberly in a steam bath.

ALICE. Right. Won't take long.

LEORA. One more check of the technical details on that bomb and the book goes to Angie. *(Others have gone and she looks around)* Beach bum? Hah! Irene Smithfield? Hah again! Sarah Trent, I wish you were real.

(Exits her room.)
(After a moment PHOEBE pokes her head in the windows. She is holding a copy of 'The Mail Is Black' and a felt tip pen.)

PHOEBE. Yoo-hoo. Yoo-hoo. *(Sees no one is there)* Bother. *(Hears something, goes to door U.L. and listens)* Beeps from a lap top. Sarah Trent is working. *(Goes to desk, opens drawers)* Maybe I could take a pencil or a pen, some memorabilia. *(Stops and turns to door R.)* What's that? Pacing and mumbling. Sarah Trent thinking aloud? Then who is in there? *(Looks U.L.)* Secretary. Must be her secretary. *(Picks up the clock)* Eleven-thirty. *(Looks at clock)* Tiffany, ha! I don't care what's stamped on it. Korea, definitely Korea.

(KENNETH MILLER has stood in arch during last bit. He is in his forties, nice looking and very well dressed.)

KEN. Excuse me.
PHOEBE. Oh, dear, I am not a burglar. The door was open.
KEN. I know. Should I ask if you have the time?
PHOEBE. *(She is holding the clock and he goes to her)* Why, yes, right here.
KEN. You're holding a clock and I thought it the right thing to say.
PHOEBE. *(Puts clock down, goes C. with book held out)* I've come for Sarah Trent's autograph.
KEN. She is here then?
PHOEBE. She's working in one of these rooms.
KEN. Leave the book with me and I'll see she signs it.
PHOEBE. You can do that?
KEN. Of course.
PHOEBE. You work for her?
KEN. Hardly. I am Sarah Trent's husband.

PHOEBE. I didn't know. She never mentioned a husband in 'The Mail Is Black'.

KEN. After the attack. We met in the hospital.

PHOEBE. How romantic. You're a doctor?

KEN. Patient. I had my gall bladder out.

PHOEBE. It's still sort of romantic.

KEN. *(He takes the book and guides her to the arch)* Let me keep this and I'll see it gets signed. Who shall she make it out to?

PHOEBE. Phoebe, Phoebe Baxter. I'm the real estate agent for this house. *(Takes the book back)* No, I must see her sign it personally. I'll come back later. *(Turns in arch)* Does Sarah Trent know you're coming or are you a surprise?

KEN. *(As both go out arch)* I am definitely a surprise.

PHOEBE. *(Off stage)* How exciting.

KEN. *(Off stage)* I do hope so. *(He comes back in, cases the room, goes to the desk, looks on top, picks up clock)* She's right, Korea.

(Hears something in room R. and knocks on door.)

ALICE. *(Off stage)* One minute, almost finished.

LEORA. *(Off stage after KEN knocks on her door)* I've got the bomb defused. Crossed terminals.

DD. *(Off stage after KEN knocks on her door)* The dianthus is out. I'm planting portulaca.

KEN. *(Looks between all rooms)* Which is she? Which? *(Goes C. and calls loudly)* Sarah! Sarah Trent! *(After three beats all doors open and the girls' heads pop out)* Which of you is Sarah Trent?

ALICE, LEORA & DD. Not me! Her!

(Point at each other and close doors.)
(Curtain)

ACT II

Scene One

(That evening after dinner. French windows are closed and locked. Coffee pot and 1 cup is on table C. DD holds a cup and looks out windows. LEORA with a cup sits in the chair L.)

DD. Water, water everywhere.

LEORA. That's what an ocean is.

DD. Nothing else. No Angela Plunkett, no Irene Smithfield and most of all no Mr. Sarah Trent.

LEORA. He must be the blackmailer.

DD. *(Goes above table)* But he could be with the FBI or CIA or one of those lettered agencies.

LEORA. Anyway, he obviously didn't know there were three Sarah Trents.

DD. He certainly ran away fast. If he was a white hat then wouldn't he know about us three?

LEORA. According to Angie we are a better kept secret than Dracula's resting place.

DD. *(Sits by her on the hassock)* Then why did he run?

LEORA. Confusion. He comes to see Sarah Trent for whatever reason and suddenly three doors open and three, oh so charming ladies pop out and won't admit which she is.

DD. He must be regrouping his thoughts.

LEORA. But he'll return to settle his business whether he's a white or a black hat.

DD. *(Rises and pours coffee in her cup)* Is this better than our writing?

LEORA. No way.

DD. But with fifty thousand dollars, a blackmail note and this place peppered with good and bad people I think it is suspenseful.

LEORA. *(Holds up cup for DD who comes and fills it)* But not like our Kimberly when she enters the living room and all the curtains are still billowing so she knows someone has just left.

DD. I get goose bumps whenever I go over that part.

(Pot back on table.)

LEORA. You didn't mind my blue penciling that long bit about the pattern of the drapes, did you?

DD. *(Sits L. of table)* No, I got carried away. It did cut down the build. Thanks.

LEORA. Don't thank me. It's what we each do so well. Was I upset when you cut out my detailed description of Kimberly's speedboat when the motor had been tinkered with?

DD. Yes, you were.

LEORA. But only temporarily.

DD. I thought just 'tinkered' was explanation enough.

LEORA. I do get too technical, don't I?

DD. And I get too flowery.

LEORA. And Alice gets a mite too descriptive. She'd better stop or we'll be X-rated.

ALICE. *(Comes in from her room with a pile of typed pages which she puts on the desk and crosses C.)* Book-of-the-Month, a major motion picture, I can see it now.

LEORA. *(Laughs)* We're too much.

DD. *(Pours coffee for ALICE)* What do you mean?

LEORA. We three sit here with out finished book and all agree it is stupendous. We're not reviewers. What do we know?

DD. Killjoy.

ALICE. If we don't like it why should we expect anyone else to?

DD. I can't wait to get started on the next one.

ALICE. *(Sits R. of table)* Not about blackmailers, please.

DD. If this new one sells as well as 'The Mail Is Black' I'm going to quit my job.

ALICE. Aha, you have a job. Then you're not a fussy homebody.

LEORA. She may be a fussy decorator. You know, window treatments and all that.

DD. You're both wrong. I can't wait to tell you what I really am.

ALICE. Me, too. I'll surprise both of you.

LEORA. *(Rises and goes to windows)* Not me. I am what I am and that's it.

ALICE. But you have hidden agenda we know naught of.

DD. Still water runs deep.

LEORA. *(Goes above table)* Oh, another original thought from DD.

(Front door bell rings.)

DD. What's that?

LEORA. I assume a bell.

DD. *(Rises)* Someone's here.

LEORA. But who?

ALICE. You're sure the door is locked?

LEORA. Doors and windows locked, bolted, and I may even have hung some garlic on the knobs.

ALICE. *(Rises)* Should we answer it?

LEORA. It could be the blackmailer.

DD. Do they usually ring the front doorbell?

ALICE. We don't have the fifty thousand to give him.

DD. Suppose it's the Prize Patrol and we've won millions?

LEORA. *(Goes to arch)* I'll go see who it is.

ALICE. If you're not back in three minutes I'm calling 911.

DD. *(To LEORA)* It is a far, far better thing you do now.

LEORA. That was Sidney Carton being guillotined. I'm only answering the door.

(Exits)

DD. *(Goes to windows)* If she screams I'll run for help.

ALICE. I took a Red Cross First Aid course. I can bandage.

DD. Guillotines need very large bandages.

ALICE. *(As ANGIE appears in the windows behind DD. She has her briefcase)* Look out!

(ANGIE knocks on windows causing a yelp from DD.)

DD. *(Turns)* It's Angie Plunkett. My heart stopped.

ALICE. I also do CPR.

DD. *(Unlocks and opens windows)* Someone's at the front door.

ANGIE. Me. I rang the bell but no one answered.

LEORA. *(Comes rushing in from hall)* No one there and – oh, it's only you.

ANGIE. I have always hated that line.

ALICE. In movies girls always say, 'Oh, it's only you' when it is obvious who it is.

LEORA. Unless the camera doesn't show who it is and then the girl is strangled.

ALICE. *(Sits on bench)* If you've come for the finished book we have it.

ANGIE. *(Goes to her)* Where?

LEORA. It's still in three parts but we've each gone over everything and you can have it tomorrow.

ANGIE. Good.

LEORA. *(Sits on hassock)* So much for fiction, now for real life.

ALICE. What should we do, quietly steal away like the fog on tiny cat feet?

DD. *(Goes above table)* You stole that.

ALICE. I rewrote it.

ANGIE. You three Sarah Trents have a million dollars in publicity being handed to you.

LEORA. That's three hundred and thirty three thousand each.

ALICE. Plus a few dollars.

ANGIE. All we have to do is catch this blackmailer.

LEORA. But how?

DD. Aye, there's the rub.

ALICE. Don't you ever say anything original?

DD. *(Sits table L.)* If someone else has said it better why try to top it?

ANGIE. About this problem here. We know there is a blackmailer prowling about with Irene's note.

LEORA. Right.

ANGIE. *(Goes above table)* We also know the sand dunes are alive with the sound of government agents.

DD. But how do we know which is which?

ANGIE. We don't have to. The blackmailer is coming here tonight to exchange the note for the money that Sarah Trent has. It can all be done without us.

ALICE. How?

ANGIE. *(Goes to table R.)* All Sarah Trent has to do is let everyone know the money is being brought here at – what, midnight?

LEORA. Too obvious.

ANGIE. Then one A.M. *(Goes below table to LEORA)* Since everyone will know and be here, the good one can arrest the bad one, Irene can get her note and money and that's it.

ALICE. And we get a finder's fee.

DD. Once again, from the top, please.

ANGIE. *(Goes above table)* You let anyone who comes snooping around for any reason know that something big will happen at one o'clock, but be subtle.

DD. Subtle I am not good at.

ALICE. You say Sarah Trent should tell everyone but which Sarah Trent?

ALICE. *(Rises)* Acting? I am good at acting. I once took a course in The Method acting but –

LEORA. Alice, quiet! Nothing about yourself, remember.

ALICE. *(Goes to R. of desk and sits)* Sorry, but I could play Sarah Trent.

DD. So we hint subtly that the money will be here at one A.M.

LEORA. I hope the FBI is as clever as the blackmailer.

DD. Maybe he'll wear a black hat.

ALICE. What if something goes wrong and all that money is here and the wrong person picks it up?

ANGIE. Fake. *(Puts case on table and removes same envelope and takes out paper with bills on the outside)* You remember it was in large bills, but now it is in two large bills wrapped around torn newspaper.

ALICE. It's bound to go wrong.

ANGIE. Why?

ALICE. It's too stupid to work.

LEORA. That's what the Trojans said about that wooden horse.

DD. We know all about the Greeks bearing gifts.

LEORA. Angie, where is the rest of the money?

ANGIE. *(Goes to LEORA at L.)* That is my secret till this is over.

IRENE. *(Rushes in French windows)* Help! The money is gone! Angela Plunkett is gone! The money is gone! *(Sees ANGIE)* Oh, there you are.

ANGIE. *(Holds up the envelope and puts it back in case)* Here I am with the money.

IRENE. Did he show up? Do you have the note?

ANGIE. Not yet.

DD. But at one A.M.

IRENE. What at one A.M.?

DD. *(Rises and goes to LEORA)* We know that's when the exchange will take place.

IRENE. How do you know?

ALICE. She is Sarah Trent.

IRENE. You?

DD. So they tell me.

IRENE. *(Goes below table to DD)* What do you mean about one o'clock?

DD. Well –

LEORA. *(Rises)* Sarah Trent cannot reveal her methods.

IRENE. *(To LEORA)* Then you must be Sarah Trent's secretary.

LEORA. You guessed it. I put the golden words onto a silver disc.

IRENE. And this is Sarah's sister. *(Goes to R. of table)* Alice Trent.

ALICE. *(Rises)* Yes, that's me. How do you do?

IRENE. *(Crosses to desk)* You weren't mentioned in the book.

ALICE. We were estranged but the book brought us very close together.

DD. Very close indeed.

IRENE. *(Turns to ANGIE)* I must be here for the exchange. Where shall I hide?

ANGIE. It's several hours yet.

IRENE. Should I change? Yes, something dark, more nondescript. I'll redo my hair. I mustn't be recognized by anyone.

DD. Yes, you do that. As Sarah Trent I have donned many disguises.

IRENE. *(To windows)* It's quite dark out here.

LEORA. That happens at night even on the beach.

IRENE. *(To ANGIE)* Aren't you coming back to the B and B?

ANGIE. Well, I –

LEORA. Perhaps it would be better if we were left alone to put everything in motion.

IRENE. Should we leave the money here?

DD. Do you mistrust Sarah Trent?

IRENE. Sorry, I wasn't thinking.

ANGIE. *(Taking IRENE to the windows with the briefcase)* Come along, Irene. I have the money with us. I'll help you change your hair style.

IRENE. *(As they disappear)* I should have brought a wig.

ALICE. *(Goes to R. of desk)* You mean that isn't a wig?

DD. My sofa is covered with better material.

LEORA. If we're expecting company at one o'clock I'd better unlock the front door again.

(Goes out arch.)

ALICE. And leave it standing open like an invitation.

DD. Suppose no one shows up?

ALICE. *(Crosses below table)* The blackmailer will have to. He wants his money.

DD. *(Goes to her)* Then we get the note.

ALICE. And you give it to Irene.

DD. Me?

ALICE. She thinks you're Sarah Trent.

DD. I'm only one third. I don't know if I can pull off the other two thirds.

(Stifled scream from LEORA off stage.)

ALICE. Leora!

LEORA. *(Off stage)* Oh, it's only you.

DD. People really do say that line.

ALICE. *(Goes below table and calls)* Leora, who is it?

LEORA. *(Enters)* Guess who's here.

ALICE. I can't.

OSSIE. *(Enters behind LEORA)* Hi, there. It's me again.

DD. Oh, it's only you. *(ALICE glares at her)* Pretend I never said it.

OSSIE. *(Goes to ALICE)* I have something for you.

ALICE. I think I know what it is.

OSSIE. I bet you're that Sarah Trent everyone is talking about.

DD. *(Sits on bench as LEORA goes L. of chair L.)* Yes, she is Sarah Trent. Yes, sir, she is the one.

LEORA. Who is talking about Sarah Trent?

OSSIE. Getting the wine, they say mystery writer up here.

ALICE. You've come early. I don't have what you want yet.

LEORA. But she will have it at one o'clock.

ALICE. Special messenger is bringing it. Dead of night. No one will suspect. No chance of a robbery.

OSSIE. You're a mystery writer all right.

ALICE. You're confused?

OSSIE. I can't wait till one o'clock so let me give it to you now.

ALICE. You trust me that much?

DD. An honest crook. Incredible.

OSSIE. Here it is.

(Reaches in his pocket. DD rises.)

ALICE. The note?

LEORA. *(Goes below chair L.)* I don't believe this. I would never write it.

ALICE. And if you did I would blue pencil it.

OSSIE. *(Still searching his pockets)* It's in here somewhere.

DD. He's lost the note.

OSSIE. No, here it is. *(Pulls out a handkerchief with change in it)* Put out your hand.

(ALICE does and he puts the change into it.)

ALICE. But the note?

OSSIE. No bills. Just change.

LEORA. That is change from the tip?

OSSIE. I got a cheap wine.

DD. He *is* honest.

OSSIE. *(Goes below ALICE to DD)* Beach Bums can be honest and millionaires can be crooks.

LEORA. A philosophizing beach bum. I didn't know they existed outside of Joseph Conrad.

DD. Life is stranger than fiction. *(They glare at her as she sinks on bench)* I know, it's been said before.

KEN. *(In windows with revolver pulled out, comes in and goes L.)* OK! Hold it right there! No one move!

LEORA. I wouldn't think of it.

OSSIE. It's a hold-up.

KEN. *(Goes L. of table to OSSIE)* You should know. It's all right now. *(To ALICE)* You're safe. *(Pulls ALICE behind him)* And you're under arrest.

OSSIE. For what?

KEN. Robbery.

DD. But he's honest.

ALICE. He's not taking money, he's returning it.

KEN. But I thought –

LEORA. Maybe you shouldn't have. This man deserves a medal. He is an honest beach bum.

DD. *(Rises)* And might we ask who you are. The last time we saw you you claimed to be Sarah Trent's husband.

KEN. I lied.

ALICE. Now you're being honest.

KEN. *(To OSSIE)* And I apologize to you, sir. I was just walking on the beach when I happened to glance in and –

LEORA. Happened to?

KEN. On purpose. I am with the Federal Bureau of Investigation.

OSSIE. A copper.

ALICE. How colloquial.

LEORA. But why did you come in before?

KEN. *(Goes to her)* I'm on a case and Sarah Trent knows why I am here. I was trying to locate her but three of you answered. Now let's have it. Which of you is Sarah Trent?

OSSIE. *(Points to ALICE)* She is.

DD. No. *(Points to LEORA)* That is Sarah Trent.

LEORA. Goody. It is my turn.

KEN. *(To her)* Then you know why I am here.

LEORA. Yes, of course.

KEN. Has it happened yet?

LEORA. No.

OSSIE. It will happen at one o'clock whatever it is.

KEN. How do you know that?

OSSIE. *(To ALICE)* She told me.

KEN. But she is not Sarah Trent.

OSSIE. Isn't she? *(Indicates LEORA)* Maybe that one is lying.

KEN. Are you?

LEORA. Maybe.

ALICE. There are too many people here for anything to happen.

LEORA. Yes. *(To OSSIE)* You should go get another wine and *(To KEN)* you should hide out on the dunes.

KEN. You must be Sarah Trent. You know just what to do. *(Goes to OSSIE)* Come along, we'll leave these ladies alone for awhile.

OSSIE. Then I'm not under arrest?

KEN. *(Goes to windows)* If we arrested everyone who returned money the jails would be empty. Come on.

ALICE. Thank you very much for the money, Mr. – er – Bum.

OSSIE. *(Smiles)* I'll be seeing you.

(Exits)

ALICE. *(Goes to KEN)* Just a minute. You come in here waving a gun but how do we know you are with the FBI?

LEORA. Good point. How do we know?

KEN. *(Smiles)* You don't.

(Exits)

ALICE. *(Goes above table)* Is he or isn't he?

DD. *(Sits on the bench)* With the government?

LEORA. *(Goes to table L.)* And what about that beach bum? Who returns money?

ALICE. I do and I'm no bum. *(They look at her)* You'll just have to take my word for it.

DD. Anyway, at one o'clock the guilty one shows up.

LEORA. *(Sits L. of table)* And, we hope, the detective to arrest him.

ALICE. Is that everyone?

LEORA. Who else?

DD. If I were writing this someone would come in and say, 'Here I am'.

ALICE. I strongly doubt if that will happen.

PHOEBE. *(In arch)* Here I am.

ALICE. I erase my doubt.

PHOEBE. *(Comes into room and sees all three)* I'm so sorry. I thought Angela Plunkett would be here.

LEORA. She's at that B and B down the beach.

PHOEBE. She said Sarah Trent would be here.

LEORA. She is.

PHOEBE. It's you. *(Charges on her)* I am so honored. I am Phoebe from the office.

LEORA. I am Leora from out of state.

PHOEBE. *(Goes to her)* I'm sorry but you look exactly like Sarah Trent should.

DD. You can't tell a book by its cover.

ALICE. *(Sarcastically)* What a good line.

PHOEBE. *(Goes below table to DD)* Then it's you. You're so modest. You are Sarah Trent.

ALICE & LEORA. Right.

DD. You guessed it.

PHOEBE. You were working before but now I am back and I have it with me.

DD. *(Rises)* You do?

PHOEBE. *(Digs into her large bag)* Right in here.

DD. Then I know what you want.

PHOEBE. This is so exciting.

DD. *(Goes below desk to R. of it)* But it won't be here till one o'clock.

PHOEBE. This morning?

DD. It's being delivered.

PHOEBE. But I have one right here. *(Brings out pen)* It's a felt tip.

DD. For what?

PHOEBE. Your autograph on 'The Mail Is Black'.

(Brings out copy.)

DD. That's why you came?

PHOEBE. Why else?

ALICE. Sign it, Sarah.

LEORA. Go ahead.

DD. We're all agreed I should?

ALICE. *(As DD sits at desk)* Yes.

LEORA. Write legibly.

DD. Here goes.

(Signs inside of book.)

PHOEBE. *(Watching awestruck)* Signed by the author. This is a first for me.

DD. *(Hands book back)* And for Sarah Trent.

LEORA. *(Covering for her)* Except at those book signing parties.

PHOEBE. *(Goes to arch)* I'll just run along and let you visit with your friends.

ALICE. We have a lot of planning to do.

PHOEBE. I can see myself out. After all I rented the place to you.

LEORA. Then you're the house agent?

PHOEBE. Who did you think I was?

LEORA. Just another Sarah Trent fan.

PHOEBE. I hope the one o'clock works out for you. An odd time for a delivery but then odd things must always happen to Sarah Trent.

(Laughs as exits.)

ALICE. *(Moves L. of table)* They certainly do.

LEORA. And they get odder by the minute.

DD. Well, as I always say, truth is –

LEORA. *(Goes to desk)* You have always said that not ten minutes ago.

DD. *(Rises)* Well, you repeat enough. If I have to read one more time where you describe hacking into a computer –

ALICE. Come on, we all repeat a bit.

DD. *(Goes to ALICE)* But it amazes me how many different ways you can describe seduction. When Kimberly –

LEORA. Perhaps it's from experience.

ALICE. My experiences will be in our next book.

DD. Not ours but Sarah Trent's. Remember she is now alive.

ALICE. Why did Angie have to say that?

LEORA. *(Sits on the bench)* To get bigger royalties, that's why.

DD. Maybe we should kill ourselves. I mean kill Sarah Trent and start over with another detective.

LEORA. We kill her? That would be killing –

DD. The goose that lays the golden egg. *(Sits R. of table)* There, you see, you do it, too.

LEORA. Listen, everyone thinks a different one of us is Sarah Trent. The blackmailer is going to deal with whichever of us he thinks she is.

ALICE. It has to be one on one. *(Sits table L.)* Who do we suspect?

LEORA. Any of them. That real estate lady, Phoebe, thinks DD is Sarah Trent. The beach bum goes for Alice.

ALICE. It's my seductive charm.

LEORA. And I get the FBI agent.

DD. If he is one.

LEORA. Right, but whoever it is will want to speak to his Sarah and alone and we three stick together like Ying and Yang.

DD. That's only two.

LEORA. Then Ying, Yang and Tang.

ALICE. *(Rises and goes above table)* I know. Let's have a falling out, a real fight then we'll be available individually.

DD. I can't fight with you girls. I don't know enough about you to get angry.

LEORA. *(Rises)* Alice has a point. We'll each storm off to our own room and then whoever it is can get to his Sarah Trent easily.

DD. At one o'clock.

LEORA. I'll set the alarm.

(Does so at desk.)

DD. It's from Tiffanys.

LEORA. *(Holds it up)* Ha!

DD. How will we do this fight?

LEORA. Alice, you took an acting course so you tell us what to do.

ALICE. My fifteen minutes of fame.

DD. How will the black hat know we fight?

LEORA. Don't be silly. He's out there now getting as close as he can to the house.

ALICE. So we have to be loud and stand quite near the windows here.

(Goes to windows.)

LEORA. *(Moves by the closet)* What shall we fight about?

ALICE. Men, what else?

DD. *(To L. of ALICE)* Yes, women are always supposed to fight over men.

ALICE. Make something up. Go ahead and be loud.

DD. *(Loud)* I heard you on the extension phone. You're after my husband.

ALICE. *(Loud)* No way. I could do better than him at the Senior Center.

LEORA. *(Loud)* And you do better with my Chauncy.

ALICE. *(Tries not to laugh. Sotto voce)* Chauncy?

LEORA. It just popped out.

DD. *(Loud)* Then you are a Jezebel and I never want to see you again.

(Slams door as she goes into her room D.L.)

ALICE. *(Loud)* That's fine with me. *(To LEORA)* And what about you?

LEORA. *(Loud)* Same for me. I think you're just a – a –

ALICE. *(Sotto voce)* Nerd.

LEORA. *(Sotto voce)* What in hell is a nerd?

ALICE. *(Sotto voce)* Get with it.

LEORA. *(Loud)* You are just a nerd and I am through.

(Slams out into her room U.L.)

ALICE. *(Loud as goes to her door D.R.)* Go on, both of you, get out of here. We are friends no longer. I never want to see either of you again.

(Slams door. In a moment all three doors open and each gives a thumbs up sign.)

LEORA. *(Whispers)* I deserve an Oscar.

DD. *(Whispers)* That was fun.

ALICE. *(Whispers)* Now we wait until –

ALL THREE. One o'clock

(Doors close as ...)
(Curtain)

Scene Two

(Later that evening. Alarm rings on desk. All poke heads out and talk in whispers.)

ALICE. I got it!

(Puts alarm off.)

LEORA. It's one o'clock already?

ALICE. I put it on for five to one so we'd be ready.

DD. *(Crosses in by chair L.)* I had a thought.

ALICE. Original?

LEORA. *(Comes down to DD)* DD has good thoughts. What is it?

DD. *(Moves below table)* We don't know each other very well so suppose one of us is not who she is supposed to be.

ALICE. You mean you don't trust me?

DD. It was just a passing thought.

LEORA. *(Crosses to her)* But now that you mention it, what do we know about you?

ALICE. *(Goes to her)* Yes, how about that?

DD. Let's drop the subject.

(Goes below ALICE to desk, LEORA to windows, and ALICE sits table R.)

ALICE. It is definitely not one of us. It's someone out there.

DD. Who will be here any minute.

LEORA. There is a shadow on the beach and it's moving this way. To our rooms!

(All rush to their rooms.)

ALICE. One scream and all three Sarah Trents will wrestle him to the ground.

DD. I don't have a black belt.

LEORA. If you did it would be paisley.

(The doors close.)

KEN. *(KEN enters windows, looks around, gets C. whispers rather loudly)* Sarah! Sarah Trent!

DD. *(Opens her door)* Yes. *(Sees it is KEN)* No!

KEN. What?

DD. Sarah Trent is in that room.

(Points U.L.)

KEN. Thanks.

(DD back into her room as he goes towards U.L. but LEORA opens her door before he gets there.)

LEORA. You called? Sarah Trent answers.

KEN. From what you said I should be here at one o'clock. It is now past that.

LEORA. But can I be sure you are a government agent? Are you genuine?

KEN. As genuine as you.

(Glances out windows.)

LEORA. That's what worries me.

KEN. There is to be a pay-off here and I want that blackmailer.

LEORA. Then you do know the whole story?

KEN. *(Goes to her)* I'm with the government. I know everything.

LEORA. That worries me even more.

KEN. I'd better hide somewhere and see who shows up for the money.

LEORA. Come in here.

KEN. I can tell my grandchildren I was in Sarah Trent's bedroom.

LEORA. *(As she pulls him into the room)* You'd only be one third correct.

(Closes the door.)
(ALICE has poked her head out and watches them disappear. Footsteps sound from the arch and ALICE goes back into her room.)

ANGIE. *(Looks into room. She has the tote bag with her. She whispers behind her.)* It's safe.

IRENE. *(Enters behind ANGIE and goes U.C.)* Sarah Trent mustn't give up the money until I have that note.

ANGIE. She won't.

IRENE. Which room is Sarah Trent in?

ANGIE. Take your choice.

IRENE. I must see her alone to make plans, somewhere we won't be overheard. *(Goes to closet and opens door)* In here. Find her and bring her to me.

ANGIE. The Sarah Trent you met earlier?

IRENE. There is only one Sarah Trent.

ANGIE. *(Goes to her)* Yes, you picked her out.

IRENE. *(Goes into the closet)* Hurry, bring her before the blackmailer shows up. *(Grabs tote bag from ANGIE)* I'd better take the money. After all, it is still mine.

(Closes the door.)

ANGIE. *(Left alone)* You keep what's in that envelope and I'll keep the rest. *(Goes to DD's door and taps lightly)* DD, it's me.

DD. *(Opens door)* Good, it's only you.

ANGIE. Who did you expect?

DD. I didn't know.

LEORA. *(Pokes head out of her room)* Angie, good, it's only you.

ANGIE. We seem agreed on that.

LEORA. Where is Irene Smithfield?

ANGIE. *(Crosses LEORA and points at closet)* In that closet.

DD. Ask a silly question –

ANGIE. She is in there. I swear by my percentage of your book.

DD. I believe you.

(Goes to closet.)

LEORA. *(To DD)* Maybe she'll tell you who the note was from.

ANGIE. Someone important I bet. Find out.

DD. *(Hand on knob, turns to LEORA)* Why don't you find out?

LEORA. Because she thinks you are Sarah Trent.

DD. Then I must act like her. *(Hand back on knob as OSSIE comes in windows)* Here I go.

OSSIE. *(Behind DD)* Hold it right there. Don't move.

(LEORA backs into her room and closes door.)

ANGIE. It's you!

DD. *(At same time with her back to him, she raises her hands)* Don't shoot!

ANGIE. He doesn't have a gun.

OSSIE. Put your hands down and none of your famous karate.

DD. *(Turns)* I don't do karate.

OSSIE. Then Sarah Trent is all a bluff?

ANGIE. You know?

DD. You've found out.

OSSIE. So you gave yourself a few attributes in the book. Who can blame you?

DD. Just a few, a very few.

OSSIE. What is so fascinating about that closet?

DD. You won't believe it.

OSSIE. What is in there?

ANGIE. Irene Smithfield.

OSSIE. From Washington?

ANGIE. You know her?

OSSIE. Of her, yes. Is she really in there? I don't believe it. *(DD opens door and IRENE stands there)* I believe it.

IRENE. I wish to see Sarah Trent alone.

DD. In just a minute.

IRENE. I'll wait right here.

(Closes the door.)

OSSIE. Irene Smithfield's not her real name.

ANGIE. We know.

DD. You suddenly seem a very different beach bum.

OSSIE. *(Goes to desk)* It's my cover. I'm with the FBI.

ANGIE. You can't be.

OSSIE. Why not?

DD. *(Glances at LEORA's door)* Isn't there another federal agent here – somewhere?

OSSIE. Not surprising. The departments thrive on jealousy, but this is my big break.

DD. *(Goes to him)* Do you have identification?

OSSIE. You're not Sarah Trent. She would know identification can be bought on any street corner in Washington.

ANGIE. *(Moves down L. of table)* He's right.

DD. *(Goes below table to her)* Yes, Sarah Trent should know that.

OSSIE. This blackmailer doesn't just pick on gossips. That's a sideline. He's the one who's been getting Pentagon secrets by blackmail and selling them for a fortune.

ANGIE. *(Moves below DD)* And he'll be here tonight.

OSSIE. You set the stage and now it's time for him to enter.

DD. Him or her.

OSSIE. You sound like an author. They always say that.

ANGIE. Yes, don't they.

OSSIE. Where is Sarah Trent?

ANGIE. *(Goes to ALICE's room)* In there. *(Knocks on door)* I'll get her out.

(Moves U.C.)

DD. Will you make an arrest this very night?

OSSIE. The moment the perp trades the note for the cash.

ALICE. *(Opens her door)* What a crowd. I must be missing something.

DD. Not too much. That Kenneth is in Leora's room, the beach bum here is with the FBI and Irene Smithfield is in that closet.

ALICE. *(Goes to OSSIE)* You're an agent?

OSSIE. Yes, Ma'am.

DD. And a polite one, too.

ALICE. And Irene Smithfield is in that closet?

DD. Yes.

ALICE. I don't believe it.

(Goes below OSSIE and opens closet door.)

IRENE. I am waiting for Sarah Trent.

(Closes door.)

ALICE. Now I believe it.

ANGIE. *(Moves above chair L.)* It's deja vu.

OSSIE. But you are Sarah Trent.

ALICE. *(Crosses above table)* You deserve an explanation.

OSSIE. Not till the blackmailer is found and he won't come in with all of us standing here.

DD. Angie, you come with me. *(They go to DD's room)* Alice, you take the beach bum – excuse me – the agent with you.

ALICE. Gladly.

(Grabs his hand and takes him into her room.)

OSSIE. I like this assignment. *(To her)* Your writing is so – what shall I say – suspenseful and passionate. Is it all true?

ALICE. I exaggerate the suspense part. *(As door closes, she says to the others)* I must take off my glasses.

DD. Alice is crossing the line between fiction and reality.

ANGIE/ *(As they go into DD's room)* That may be her reality.

IRENE. *(Opens closet door and looks out)* Where is he? Who is he? *(Goes towards windows to look out and sees someone)* Who's coming now?

(Goes back into closet.)

PHOEBE. *(Enters windows with book in hand. Whispers)* Sarah? Sarah Trent. *(Looks at all doors)* Eenie, meenie, miney, mo. *(Ends at LEORA's door and taps on it)* Sarah Trent?

LEORA. *(Opens door)* Yes, who –

PHOEBE. No, not you. I want Sarah Trent.

LEORA. *(Points to DD's door)* Yes, you think – that door.

PHOEBE. Thank you. *(LEORA closes door and PHOEBE goes and taps on DD's door)* Sarah Trent?

DD. *(Opens door and whispers)* Who is it?

PHOEBE. Phoebe Baxter.

DD. I already signed your book.

PHOEBE. *(Drops her sweet nature and becomes very businesslike)* You had better come out here and now.

DD. I think I know why.

PHOEBE. You couldn't. I played my part to the hilt.

DD. *(Goes below her to C. leaving door open)* You're not from the rental agency?

PHOEBE. I am from Washington, D.C. I am a government agent.

DD. You can't be. We already have one – no, two here.

PHOEBE. But I was sent here undercover.

ANGIE. *(Comes bursting out of DD's room. Points to LEORA's door)* So was he in there *(Points to ALICE's door)* and so was he in there.

PHOEBE. I don't believe it.

DD. You want proof? O.K. just look. *(Goes D.C. and calls)* Everyone out of the pool! Come on! Let's go! All agents in here pronto!

OSSIE. *(Enters followed by ALICE and goes below desk)* Where's the competition?

PHOEBE. Right here.

KEN. *(Comes out followed by LEORA, crosses to table L.)* Who's an agent? I was promised this job solo.

PHOEBE. Obviously they didn't trust you.

KEN. *(To OSSIE)* And what about you?

OSSIE. I was here first. I have priority.

LEORA. Stop. Enough bickering. It's obvious the perp is not going to show up now.

ANGIE. This place looks like a testimonial dinner for Elliot Ness.

ALICE. Angie's right. You'd better all go.

KEN. And leave Sarah Trent alone?

OSSIE. Sarah Trent, where?

KEN. *(Holds up LEORA's hand)* Here.

OSSIE. *(Holds up ALICE's hand)* But this is Sarah Trent.

PHOEBE. You're both lousy agents. This is Sarah Trent.

(Indicates DD.)

KEN. Let's have it. Which is Sarah Trent?

ANGIE. *(Goes above table)* Quiet, the three of you. Don't say a word.

LEORA. *(To others)* But what about you three?

DD. Yes, how do we know you're legit agents?

ALICE. That's true. It's three against three.

IRENE. *(Comes out of the closet with the money)* Make it four!

(She has dropped her silly performance and is now all business.)

ANGIE. Irene Smithfield.

IRENE. I am with the CIA.

ANGIE. Not another.

(Sits L. of table.)

KEN. This is my case.

DD. *(Sinks in chair L.)* I give up.

ALICE. I favor the beach bum.

OSSIE. Thanks.

PHOEBE. I am in charge.

LEORA. *(Loud)* All right! All right! Quiet!

(They stop talking.)

ALICE. *(Sits on the bench)* Let's all simmer down.

LEORA. We seem to have a roomful of agents here.

OSSIE. *(Moves in by bench)* And Sarah Trents.

KEN. I assume we are all here for the same reason.

IRENE. To catch this blackmailer.

DD. All of you for one small-time culprit? Is this where our tax money goes?

IRENE. *(Moves D.C.)* Not small-time, Ms. Trent, or whoever you are. This is a master criminal.

OSSIE. We know he has his hands on some classified material.

IRENE. And we can get him through the love note.

LEORA. But your mystery book and the message?

KEN. That was all a set-up, wasn't it?

IRENE. The real Irene Smithfield came to our offices as all good citizens should.

DD. Then you are not the real Irene Smithfield?

IRENE. She is nowhere as silly and stupid as I have played her. She is also not a very good author.

KEN. This is the blackmailer's M.O. First he does the small scandal bit. If Irene had paid off then he'd get her to pass on more sensitive materials from her boy friend.

ANGIE. But if Irene is holding the money who is holding the note?

OSSIE. Has anyone else been hanging around here today?

DD. No.

ALICE. No one.

KEN. Then someone in this room is the blackmailer.

(They exchange looks.)

PHOEBE. It's one of those Sarah Trents. They all say they are she but who knows which is real?

ANGIE. *(Rises and goes R. of desk)* They are all Sarah Trent, the three of them collaborate. I made up the story about her being a real person.

(Collapses on desk chair.)

OSSIE. Then one of them is the blackmailer.

DD. *(Rises)* I am no blackmailer. I work as a social director in a retirement home.

LEORA. DD, that's wonderful.

ALICE. The home is awash in chintz and pots of flowers, isn't it?

DD. And what about you, Leora?

LEORA. Library researcher for a technology company on the Coast.

DD. We were right. You have assistants to look up everything for you.

LEORA. You got it.

ANGIE. Alice, who are you? Speak up.

ALICE. Do I have to?

LEORA. Yes.

ALICE. Does no one recognize me? With my glasses off and if I loosen my hair *(She does both)* like this. Now, how about it?

KEN. No, sorry.

ANGIE. There is something –

OSSIE. Wait, I go it. In – what was it called? – think – it was – yes, 'Vampires of the Millennium.' You're an actress.

DD. I have been writing with a star.

LEORA. That's why you knew all about that Method acting.

ALICE. Autographs upon request. You can see where my career is going. That's why I want to write.

LEORA. And you played those hot love scenes you write about?

ALICE. All acting I'm afraid.

IRENE. This sounds like a talk show confessional. Now let's get down to the facts. One of us is a fake. I have the money here but who has the note?

DD. This is true suspense.

ALICE. It could be our next book.

LEORA. We can write as well as this.

PHOEBE. But the real Irene Smithfield can't. That scene of hers in the train station

(Stops dead when she realizes what she has said.)

IRENE. *(After a pause while they all understand it)* No one has read that story but me.

KEN. And me and the blackmailer.

OSSIE. When it was picked up at the post office.

ANGIE. *(Points to PHOEBE)* You!

PHOEBE. *(Pulls out revolver)* O.K. so I am not an agent and I am not a real estate lady but what I am is the person who is going to get that money. Put it on the table.

IRENE. *(As puts it on the table)* There goes my job.

OSSIE. There go all our jobs.

(PHOEBE puts envelope in purse.)

ANGIE. It's a roomful of agents. Someone do something.

PHOEBE. Just to show I'm an honest blackmailer, this is the note.

(Takes folded note from purse and holds it up with the gun in the other hand.)

LEORA. Wait! Girls, Sarah Trents, remember chapter 12 in our new book?

ALICE. You mean where –

LEORA. Exactly.

DD. Will it work?

PHOEBE. What are you talking about?

LEORA. If it doesn't then we're rotten authors and we should turn in our lap tops.

ANGIE. What are you up to?

LEORA. Here we go.

(The three girls have been spreading out on all sides of PHOEBE, ALICE to the R., LEORA above and L. and DD D.L.)

KEN. What are you doing?

OSSIE. Looks dangerous to me.

PHOEBE. One more move and I shoot.

LEORA. *(The following dialogue is just above a whisper from the girls and is almost hypnotic)* You wouldn't dare.

PHOEBE. Why not?

ALICE. Because the moment you shoot one of us the other two will jump you so you really don't have a chance.

(They keep moving in on her slowly. OSSIE starts for them but KEN gestures him to stop as he realizes what they are doing.)

PHOEBE. *(Points the gun at one and then another)* That's stupid. One of you will get shot.

DD. And then you will be up for murder.

(They keep moving slowly.)

LEORA. You wouldn't want that, would you? You see, we keep moving in and you don't know what to do.

PHOEBE. Yes, I do. I'll shoot.

ALICE. No, you won't. You can't hit us all at once.

LEORA. *(PHOEBE stands there buffaloed)* So it is much better if you *(Slowly takes the gun from her)* just give me the gun.

ALICE. *(On the other side still talking quietly)* And me the note.

(Takes it.)

DD. You can keep that money – it's mostly newspaper anyway.

LEORA. *(Turns to others)* There you are, grab her.

(Moves away above chair L.)

PHOEBE. What happened? No! Damn Sarah Trent, all of them.

(As she rushes out the windows followed by IRENE and OSSIE.)

IRENE. *(As she goes)* Promotion, here I come!

OSSIE. *(A quick turn)* Alice, you stick around. I'll be back.

(He exits.)

KEN. *(To ANGIE)* After they book her I'll meet you at the B. & B.

(Exits)

ALICE. What does that mean?

ANGIE. *(Goes below desk)* You clever authors never even guessed.

LEORA. What?

ANGIE. Ken is my husband.

LEORA. That nice man? Congratulations.

ANGIE. That's how this whole scheme came about. He was in the Washington office when the real Irene came in and he got the idea for the mixed-up mail.

ALICE. He sounds clever.

ANGIE. He is.

DD. Is anyone who he should be?

ANGIE. You three are Sarah Trent and that is who you should be.

DD. What about the money?

ANGIE. *(Takes it)* I'll give it to Ken to return and I'd better find out he is. He can't run very well, a bad knee from a shoot-out.

(Exits windows.)

LEORA. I would never believe this even if I saw it in the National Enquirer.

ALICE. *(Comes D.C.)* I seem to be holding this blackmail note.

LEORA. *(Puts gun on table)* I want to get rid of this.

DD. Should we read the note?

ALICE. Or burn it?

DD. It is a personal note from an important person.

LEORA. Burn it ... of course.

(They exchange a look and smile and rush to ALICE below table.)

ALICE. *(Reads it)* It is a love nest invitation right enough.

LEORA. Who's it from?

DD. The name is under the flap.

LEORA. Unfold it.

ALICE. *(Unfolds bottom flap of note)* It is – oh – look!

ALL THREE. *(Leans over to read the signature, then looks up)* Ohhhhhhh ...

(Curtain)

PROPERTY LIST

ACT I:

On desk:
>clock
>purse, wallet containing charge card, money clip with bills.

Off Right:
>Typed pages (Alice)

Off Left:
>Typed pages (DD)
>Tote bag with Dr. Seuss book (Phoebe)
>Sun glasses (Irene)
>Brief case with large, stuffed, stamped & addressed envelope (Angie)
>2 mugs of coffee (DD)
>Tray with 3 glasses of water (DD)
>Book titled 'The Mail Is Black' (Phoebe)
>Felt tip pen (Phoebe)

Off Up Left:
>Typed pages (Angie)

ACT II: *Scene One*

Preset:
>Coffee pot and 1 cup on table C.
>French windows closed and locked
>2 coffee cups (DD & Leora)

Off Right:
>Typed pages (Alice)
>Tote bag with same envelope & 2 bills wrapped around torn newspaper (Angie)

Off Left:
>Handkerchief with change inside (Ossie)
>Large pocketbook with felt tip pen, copy of 'The Mail Is Black' (Phoebe)

Preset:
>Strike cups, coffee pot

Off Left:
>Tote bag with envelope (Angie)
>Purse with revolver and folded note (Phoebe)

Off Right:
>Revolver (Ken)

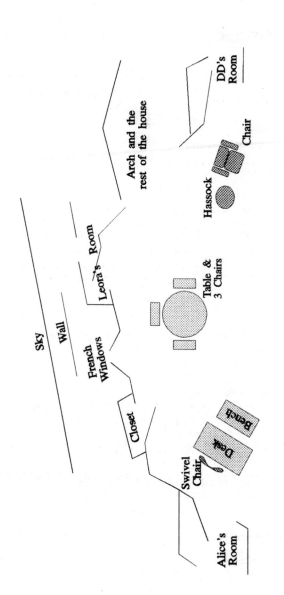

GROUND PLAN

The Trouble with Trent